Paddington

May 3, 2015

Happy 10th
Birthday~
dear Hebo~
Hope you enjoy this book,
much love,
auntie Mary Trolan

abl ۳\۹ له نه
عیر ۱،، علیّ

Paddington
Text copyright © 1998, 2007 by Michael Bond
Illustrations copyright © 2007 by R. W. Alley
Printed in the United States of America
All rights reserved. No part of this book may be used or reproduced in any manner whatsoever
without written permission except in the case of brief quotations embodied in critical articles and reviews.
For information address HarperCollins Children's Books, a division of HarperCollins Publishers,
195 Broadway, New York, NY 10007.
www.harpercollinschildrens.com

Library of Congress Cataloging-in-Publication Data is available.
ISBN-10: 0-06-117074-7 (trade bdg.) — ISBN-13: 978-0-06-117074-4 (trade bdg.)

14 15 16 PC 20 19 18 17 16 15
❖

Revised edition

First published in Great Britain by Collins, 1998
First U.S. edition, HarperCollins Publishers, 1998

MICHAEL BOND

Paddington

illustrated by R.W. ALLEY

HarperCollins*Publishers*

Mr. and Mrs. Brown first met Paddington on a railway platform. In fact, that was how he came to have such an unusual name for a bear, because Paddington was the name of the station.

The Browns were waiting to meet their daughter, Judy, when Mr. Brown noticed something small and furry near the Left Luggage office. "It looks like a bear," he said.

"A bear?" repeated Mrs. Brown. "In Paddington Station? Don't be silly, Henry. There can't be!"

But Mr. Brown was right. It was sitting on an old leather suitcase marked WANTED ON VOYAGE, and as they drew near, it stood up and politely raised its hat.

"Good afternoon," it said. "May I help you?"

"It's very kind of you," said Mr. Brown, "but as a matter of fact, we were wondering if we could help *you*?"

"You're a very small bear," said Mrs. Brown. "Where are you from?"

The bear looked around carefully before replying.

"Darkest Peru. I'm not really supposed to be here at all. I'm a stowaway."

"You don't mean to say you've come all the way from South America on your own?" exclaimed Mrs. Brown. "Whatever did you do for food?"

Unlocking the suitcase, the bear took out an almost empty glass jar. "I ate marmalade," it said. "Bears like marmalade."

Mrs. Brown looked at the label around the bear's neck.
It said, quite simply,

PLEASE LOOK
AFTER THIS
BEAR. Thank
you.

"Oh, Henry!" she cried. "We can't leave him here all by himself. There's no knowing what might happen to him. Can't he come home and stay with us?"

"Stay with us?" repeated Mr. Brown nervously.

He looked down at the bear. "Er, would you like that?" he asked. "That is," he added hastily, "if you have nothing else planned."

"Oooh, yes," replied the bear. "I would like that very much. I've nowhere to go and everyone seems in such a hurry."

"That settles it," said Mrs. Brown. "Now, you must be thirsty after your journey. Mr. Brown can get you some tea while I go and meet our daughter, Judy."

"But, Mary," said Mr. Brown. "We don't even know its name."

Mrs. Brown thought for a moment. "I know," she said. "We'll call him Paddington—after the station."

"Paddington!" The bear tested it several times to make sure. "It sounds very important."

Mr. Brown tried it out next. "Follow me, Paddington," he said. "I'll take you to the snack bar."

Mr. Brown was as good as his word. Paddington had never seen so many snacks on one tray, and he didn't know which to try first.

He was so hungry and thirsty that he climbed up onto the table to get a better look.

Mr. Brown turned away, pretending he had tea with a bear at Paddington Station every day of his life.

"Henry!" cried Mrs. Brown, when she arrived with Judy.
"What *are* you doing to that poor bear?"

Paddington jumped up to raise his hat, and in his haste,
he slipped on a strawberry tart, skidded on the cream, and
fell over backward into his cup of tea.

"I think we'd better go before anything else happens," said
Mr. Brown.

Judy took hold of Paddington's paw. "Come along," she
said. "We'll take you home, and you can meet Mrs. Bird
and my brother, Jonathan."

Mr. Brown led the way to a waiting taxi. "Number thirty-two Windsor Gardens, please," he said.

The driver stared at Paddington. "Bears is extra," he growled. "Sticky bears is twice as much. And make sure none of it comes off on my interior. It was clean when I set out this morning."

The sun was shining as they drove out of the station, and
there were cars and big red buses everywhere. Paddington
waved to some people waiting at a bus stop, and several
of them waved back. It was all very friendly.

Paddington tapped the taxi driver on his shoulder. "It isn't a bit like Darkest Peru," he announced.

The man jumped at the sound of Paddington's voice. "Cream!" he said bitterly. "Cream and jam all over my coat!" He slid the little window behind him shut.

"Oh, dear, Henry," murmured Mrs. Brown. "I wonder if we're doing the right thing?"

Fortunately, before anyone had time to answer, they arrived at Windsor Gardens, and Judy helped Paddington onto the pavement.

"Now you're going to meet Mrs. Bird," she said. "She looks after us. She's a bit fierce at times, but she doesn't really mean it. I'm sure you'll like her."

Paddington felt his knees begin to wobble. "I'm sure I shall, if you say so," he replied. "The thing is, will she like me?"

"Goodness gracious!" exclaimed Mrs. Bird. "What *have* you got there?"

"It's not a what," said Judy. "It's a bear called Paddington, and he's coming to stay with us."

"A bear," said Mrs. Bird, as Paddington raised his hat. "Well, he has good manners, I'll say that for him."

"I'm afraid I stepped on a jam tart by mistake," said
Paddington.

"I can see that," said Mrs. Bird. "You'd better have a bath
before you're very much older. Judy can turn it on for you. I
daresay you'll be wanting some marmalade, too!"

"I think she likes you," whispered Judy.

Paddington had never been in a bathroom before. While the water was running, he made himself at home. First of all, he tried writing his new name on the steam on the mirror.

Then he used Mr. Brown's shaving cream to draw a map of Peru on the floor.
It wasn't until a drip landed on his head that he remembered what he was supposed to be doing.

He soon discovered
that getting into a
bath is one thing, but
it's quite another
matter getting out
again—especially when
it's full of soapy water.

Paddington tried calling out, "Help!"— at first in a quiet voice so as not to disturb anyone, then very loudly,

"HELP!

HELP!"

When that didn't work, he began bailing the water out with his hat. But the hat had several holes in it, and his map of Peru soon turned into a sea of foam.

Suddenly Jonathan and Judy burst into the bathroom and lifted a dripping Paddington onto the floor.

"Thank goodness you're all right!" cried Judy. "We heard you calling out."

"Fancy making such a mess," said Jonathan admiringly. "You should have pulled the plug out."

"Oh!" said Paddington. "I never thought of that."

When Paddington came downstairs, he looked so clean that no one could possibly be cross with him. His fur was all soft and silky, his nose gleamed, and his paws had lost all traces of the jam and cream.

The Browns made room for him in a small armchair, and
Mrs. Bird brought him a pot of tea and a plate of hot
buttered toast and marmalade.

"Now," said Mrs. Brown, "you must tell us all about yourself. I'm sure you must have had lots of adventures."

"I have," said Paddington earnestly. "Things are always happening to me. I'm that sort of a bear." He settled back in the armchair.

"I was brought up by my aunt Lucy in Darkest Peru," he began. "But she had to go into a Home for Retired Bears in Lima." He closed his eyes thoughtfully and a hush fell over the room as everyone waited expectantly.

After a while, when nothing happened, they began to get restless. Mr. Brown tried coughing. Then he reached across and poked Paddington.

"Well, I never," he said. "I do believe he's fast asleep!"

"After all that's happened to him," said Mrs. Brown, "is it any wonder?"